This book

belongs to:

_____

_____

For Alfie & Sophie

The best kids a mama could have.

ISBN: 9798621558772

www.wafflemama.uk

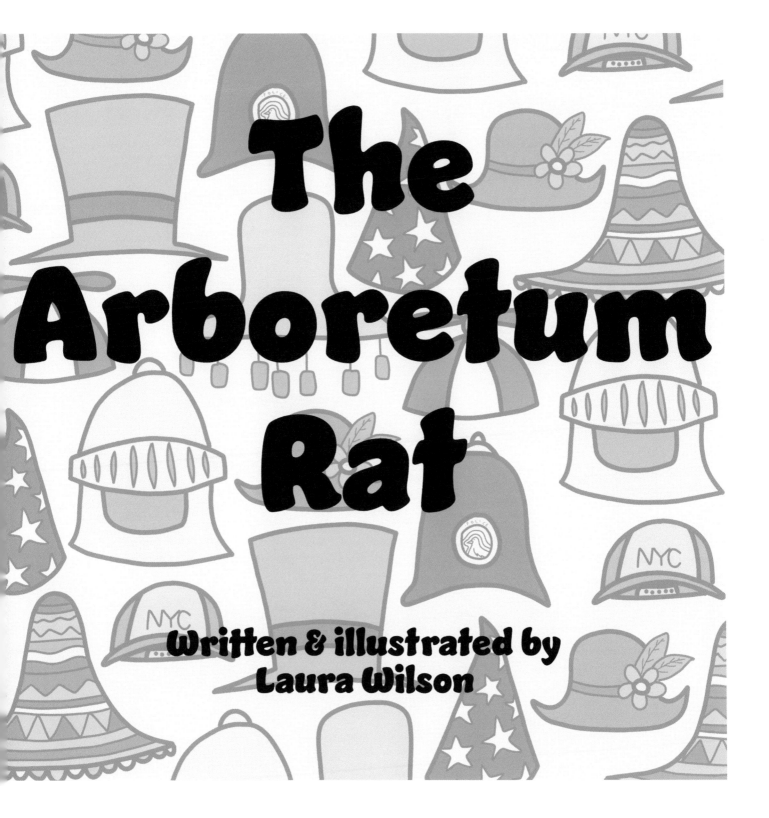

The Arboretum Rat

**Written & illustrated by
Laura Wilson**

Way out on the island there's a friendly little rat, he goes by the name of Sidney and he likes to wear a hat.

Sidney has a hundred hats,
there's one from every land.
There's even one from Egypt,
that's filled will sparkling sand!

A baseball cap from New York,
a tam from land of Scot.

A rainbow clad sombrero, a fez,
he has the lot!

On sidney's little island, there's moorhens ducks and plants.

Look a little closer and you'll see Sid's friends the ants.

The ants work hard to bring Sid food,
each and every day.

Digging up the squirrels nuts
and this is what they say...

"we ants are fans of Sidney, we like to keep him sweet. We March around the arboretum, bringing special treats."

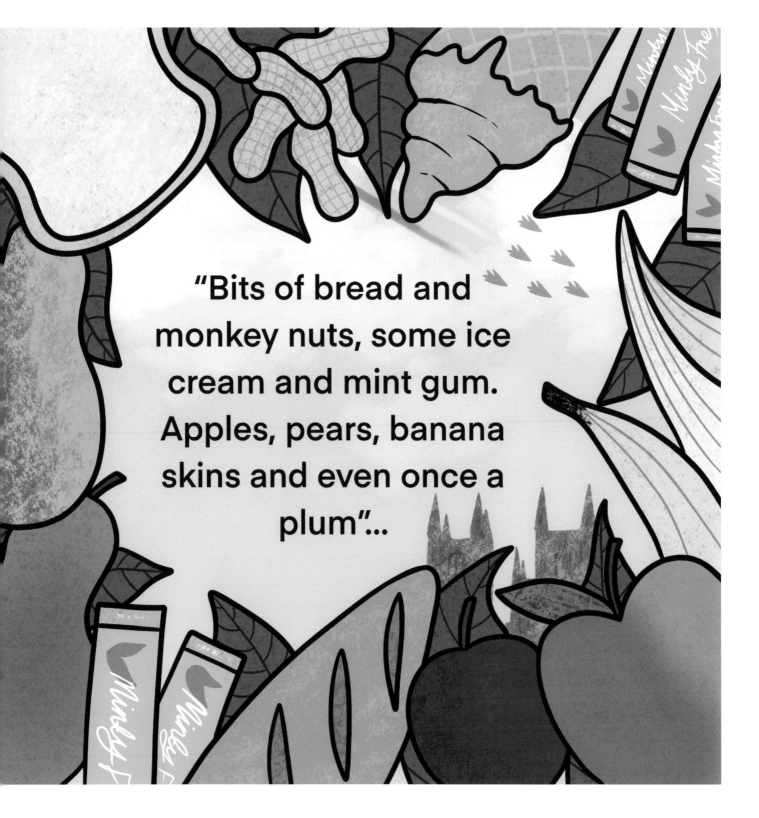

"Bits of bread and monkey nuts, some ice cream and mint gum. Apples, pears, banana skins and even once a plum"...

The ants are fans as they just said,
Sid's famous in the town.

What do you think he's famous for?
A movie star? A clown?

Well, Sidney is a busy rat, he's always in the park.

When the gates are closed at night, he sings 'til after dark.

The owls, the mice and dogs.

With backing tracks provided by the best beatboxing frogs.

You may have heard him singing in the day time or the night.

On windy days he sings up high,
way up on his kite!

They fly away in winter and bring back hats as gifts!

So now you all know Sidney and how he got his hats...

He really is the
number one, the
best of all the rats!

Printed in Great Britain
by Amazon

35894969R00021